Dear Parent:

Congratulations! Your child is taking the first steps on an exciting journey. The destination? Independent reading!

STEP INTO READING® will help your child get there. The program offers five steps to reading success. Each step includes fun stories and colorful art. There are also Step into Reading Sticker Books, Step into Reading Math Readers, Step into Reading Phonics Readers, Step into Reading Write-In Readers, and Step into Reading Phonics Boxed Sets—a complete literacy program with something to interest every child.

Learning to Read, Step by Step!

Ready to Read   Preschool–Kindergarten
• big type and easy words • rhyme and rhythm • picture clues
For children who know the alphabet and are eager to begin reading.

Reading with Help   Preschool–Grade 1
• basic vocabulary • short sentences • simple stories
For children who recognize familiar words and sound out new words with help.

Reading on Your Own   Grades 1–3
• engaging characters • easy-to-follow plots • popular topics
For children who are ready to read on their own.

Reading Paragraphs   Grades 2–3
• challenging vocabulary • short paragraphs • exciting stories
For newly independent readers who read simple sentences with confidence.

Ready for Chapters   Grades 2–4
• chapters • longer paragraphs • full-color art
For children who want to take the plunge into chapter books but still like colorful pictures.

STEP INTO READING® is designed to give every child a successful reading experience. The grade levels are only guides. Children can progress through the steps at their own speed, developing confidence in their reading, no matter what their grade.

Remember, a lifetime love of reading starts with a single step!

Visit us on the Web!
StepIntoReading.com
www.randomhouse.com/kids

Educators and librarians, for a variety of teaching tools, visit us at
www.randomhouse.com/teachers

ISBN: 978-0-375-86936-5 (trade) — ISBN: 978-0-375-96936-2 (lib. bdg.)

Printed in the United States of America

10 9 8 7 6 5 4 3 2 1

STEP INTO READING®   STEP 3

Leader of the Pack

Adapted by Jason Gots

Based on the episode "Leader of the Pack" by Alexx Van Dyne

Illustrated by Ethen Beavers

Random House 🏠 New York

Rex is a young hero
with amazing powers.
He can generate machines
from his body!

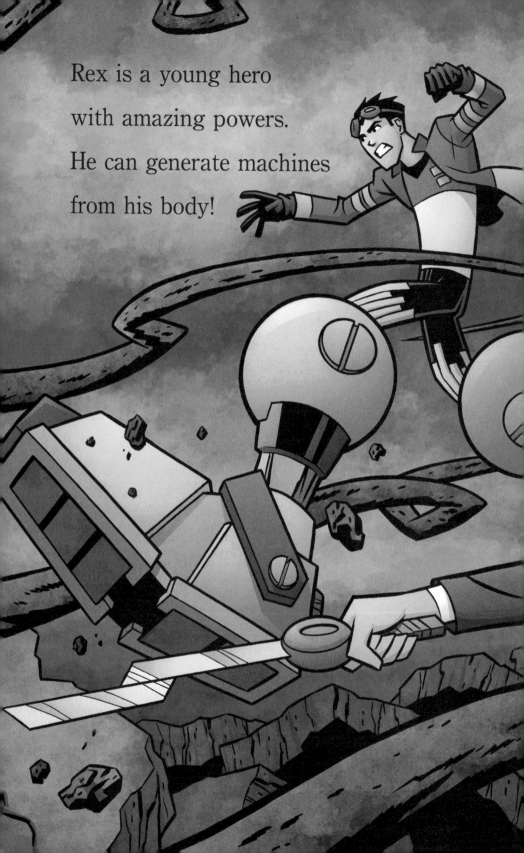

Rex and his teammates,
Bobo Haha and Agent Six,
fight monsters called Evos.

A giant Evo ship flies
over New York City.
Rex gets ready
for battle.

The villain Van Kleiss
steps out of the Evo.
Skalamander and Biowulf
stand guard.

Van Kleiss says he wants
to make peace with humans.

Agent Six tells Rex
not to fight.

Dr. Holiday is a scientist
at Rex's home base.
Dr. Holiday, Six, and Rex look at
a party invitation from Van Kleiss.

Rex says that Van Kleiss

is up to no good.

Rex and his friends
go to the party.
Dr. Holiday scans for nanites.
They are tiny robots
that turn living things
into Evos!

Rex and Bobo sneak out
to investigate.
Rex finds Circe.
She is Rex's friend,
but she works for Van Kleiss!

Pow! Circe knocks Rex out!

Bobo is captured, too.

Rex and Bobo are locked
into a prison cell.

Rex kicks down the door
with his Punkbuster boots!

Rex and Bobo find
a secret tunnel.
It is full of nanites!

An earthworm Evo attacks!

Rex and Bobo go deeper
into the tunnel.

Circe and an Evo named Breach are spreading dirt full of nanites under New York City!

The nanite dirt fuels
Van Kleiss's Evo powers.
"No way!" Rex says.
"I will stop him!"

Circe orders a worm
to attack Rex and Bobo!

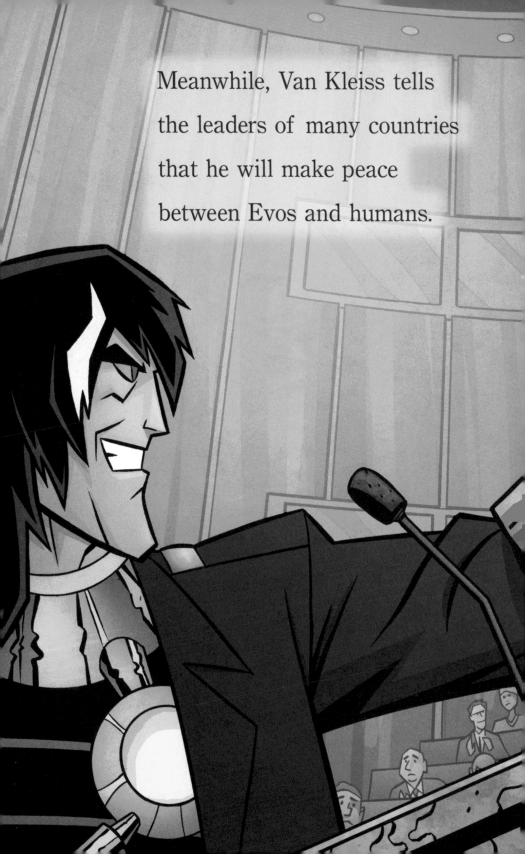

Meanwhile, Van Kleiss tells the leaders of many countries that he will make peace between Evos and humans.

The people clap,
but something is wrong.

An Evo worm crashes
through the floor.
It lifts Van Kleiss
into the air.

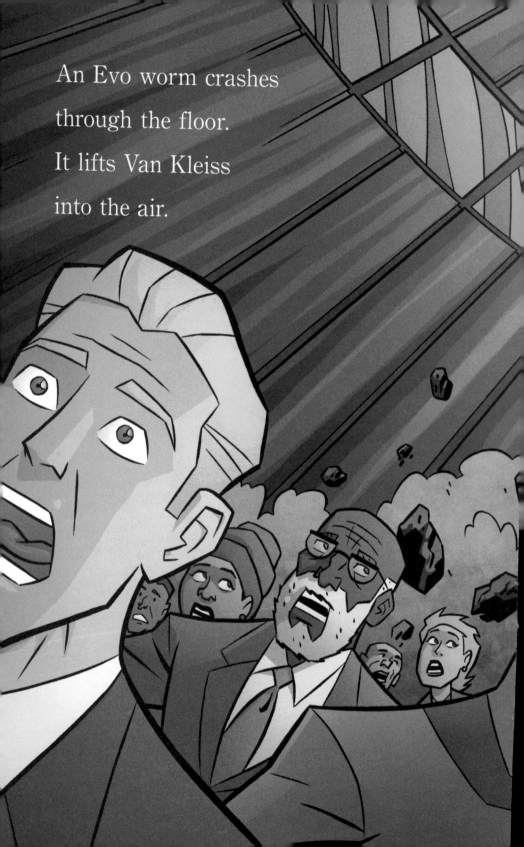

Van Kleiss tells the people
that he wants
to rule the world!

Van Kleiss makes thick vines
grow over the building!
Agent Six slashes the vines.

The vines grow back!

The people are trapped!

Rex flies into the room!

He grabs Van Kleiss

and smashes through a wall!

Van Kleiss uses his powers
to trap Rex.

The nanite dirt makes the plants grow out of control.

The plants take
over the city!

Rex escapes.
He jumps down
a manhole.

Rex smashes
the underground walls.
River water floods
the tunnel!

Rex and the nanite dirt
get washed into a river.
A worm swims away.

Rex swims to the surface
of the river.

Van Kleiss is waiting.

Rex and Van Kleiss fight!
Van Kleiss thinks
he is winning.

Van Kleiss asks Rex
to join him.
Rex says, "Never!"

As the nanite dirt washes away,

the vines dry up and die.

Van Kleiss loses his power.

Rex has stopped his plan.

"Your parents would be proud," Van Kleiss says. Rex is shocked. He cannot remember his parents.

What does Van Kleiss

know about Rex's past?

It is a trick!

The Evo ship returns.

It knocks Rex down.

Agent Six, Dr. Holiday,
and Bobo are happy
to see Rex.

Rex has saved
the city.
The people cheer!

Rex soars into the air!
He knows that a hero's work
is never done.